HALLOWEEN COSTUME party!

Uncle Amon

Uncle Amon Books
www.UncleAmon.com

Tonight is the Halloween costume party!

"I'll be a skeleton," says Marty.

"My bony skull mask will scare my friends.

The Halloween fun will never end!"

On into the evening, just after dark,

It's finally time for the party to start.

Marty's friend ,Benjamin, welcomes him in,

His eyes peeking out from a big pumpkin's grin!

There are candies and cookies and fun treats galore,

While boys and girls wearing costumes play games on the floor.

Samantha, who's dressed as a Halloween ghost,

Raises her glass for a Halloween toast!

Arnie's a monster, and everyone laughs,

As he makes cardboard claws at the table of crafts.

"You'd better watch out, or I'll get you!" he screams,

And he chases his friends – hope they won't have bad dreams!

Little Billy is dressed like a baby tonight,

Since his own baby sister sure gives him a fright!

"Goo-goo-ga-ga!" he screeches and his friends think it's funny!

They watch Billy scoot through the room on his tummy.

Elizabeth's an angel, and no one's surprised.

Her beautiful costume's a delight to the eyes.

"Look out below!" Elizabeth cries,

Flapping her wings like she's up in the skies.

Her little brother Jake is a big-headed mummy,

With bandages covering his face, legs, and tummy.

"It's sure hard to eat in this costume," he remarks,

Stuffing his face with some big chocolate bars!

Su Lin is a witch, with a flowing black dress,

And a pointy black hat that is sure to impress.

"All I need is broomstick," the little witch cries,

"And I'd soar past the rooftops, way up in the sky!"

"I may not be a broom," says Marcia the cat.

"But every witch needs a pet, so I could be that!

We'd do magic spells, turning people into trees,

And pulling funny pranks wherever we please!"

"Well, I have a broomstick," brags Sara Marie,

Who's also a witch at this festive party.

"I guess we could share," answers Su Lin with a smile,

"We'll take turns flying it every ten miles!"

Then the party guests hear a mom's car in the drive,

And they see that their friend Frankie has arrived.

"I was just trick-or-treating, and look at my treats!"

The Frankie monster cries, "Why, I'm loaded with sweets!"

"As if there aren't enough sweets in this house!"

Laughs Mandy the zombie in her sickly-green blouse.

But just the same, all the friends gather around,

To admire Frankie's candy from all over town!

After Frankie arrives, more friends show up,

In extravagant costumes, face paint, and makeup.

Jilly is dressed as a jack-o-lantern queen,

Even her hair is pumpkin-stem green!

When Margo arrives, there is one more pet cat,

And the two Halloween witches can't argue with that.

"Meow, meow!" Margo the cat purrs,

Looking just like a kitty in her cozy gray furs.

Jake's surprised to see that there's one more mummy,

It's his best friend Derek, and his costume's not crummy!

The bandages cover him from head to toe,

But his twinkly blue eyes show even so!

Last but not least, arrives Eric the ghost,

Joining the group in one more Halloween toast.

"To Halloween parties!" the good friends all shout.

"Now, this is what Halloween's all about!"

About the Author

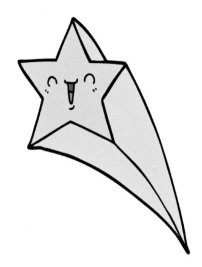

Uncle Amon began his career with a vision. It was to influence and create a positive change in the world through children's books by sharing fun and inspiring stories.

Whether it is an important lesson or just creating laughs, Uncle Amon provides insightful stories that are sure to bring a smile to your face! His unique style and creativity stand out from other children's book authors, because he uses real life experiences to tell a tale of imagination and adventure.

"I always shoot for the moon. And if I miss? I'll land in the stars."
-Uncle Amon

For more books by Uncle Amon, please visit:
www.UncleAmon.com

Made in the USA
Columbia, SC
14 October 2020

22833861R00022